MATE FOR THE SPACE COWBOY

MATCH MADE IN SPACE

PHOEBE BELLE

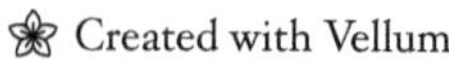 Created with Vellum

Chapter One

MELODY

Four months ago

"Melody!" My brother shouts my name.

I'm jolted with a familiar sense of fear and panic. It rises in a wave that crashes over me. I know what's coming. He storms into my apartment, the only place I've ever had any privacy. It was only after my father finally died that I was able to escape and live on my own.

My brother, who once commiserated with me over how much we hated our father and his violence, has essentially become him.

"What is it?" I ask, hating the sense of resignation I feel.

"I need money," he demands.

"I don't have any." My words come out flat and tired.

My brother, John, spins in a circle, his eyes darting around my one-room apartment.

"You have this." He swings his arm in an arc.

"You know how this works," I point out. "My apartment comes with my job. I eat meals at work."

This is true, and I feel lucky. My abusive father died in a

factory fire, and my mother had died from what we thought was cancer before that.

My brother spins back toward the door, stopping a few feet away from me before slapping me hard across the face and grabbing my arm as he shakes me. "Find me one of your friends," he demands.

I roll my eyes. "I don't have any friends, John. I go to work, and I come home and sleep."

John looks tired. I worry about him, but there is nothing I can do. All I can do is try to take care of myself.

Three days later, I learn that my brother has died in a fight. Even though he gave me nothing and became as cruel as my father, I still grieve the loss. He was my only family, the only person who knew the life we had together growing up, and the only person who missed my mother as much as I still do.

The days pass, and I keep walking to work. Every day is hot, and the dust swirls in the dry air. I'm just existing. One afternoon, I'm quietly filing paperwork in the factory. I don't even know if what I'm filing matters, but I do it anyway. At the very least, it passes the time. I have a small phone that comes with my job where I can look at Galaxy Cosmo, our planet's only social media. I scroll through it as I file with one hand in my little cubicle. My eyes land on a post.

"That can't be real," I whisper to myself.

You learn to whisper around here or try to keep your thoughts to yourself.

I reread the post. *Mates wanted. Females only. You can leave Earth forever and mate with space cowboys.*

I check the time for the interviews listed on the announcement. It's a few minutes after the end of my shift. I'll be tired, but it's a chance. A chance I might never get again.

Leaving Earth is nearly impossible unless you have *a lot* of money. Intergalactic travel isn't new, but it's rare and costly for humans on Earth. We've destroyed our planet. Aliens from other planets don't really want to visit here except out of curiosity. We know from the history books that once upon a time, Earth was the envy of the galaxy. Those days are long gone, and nothing more than dust motes in the distant past.

Now, if you live here, you hope for a job and food. Lucky people live in the green zone. Even then, we hear rumors of how horribly women are treated there. Women are second-class citizens on Earth. They stripped our rights. We're the equivalent of indentured servants.

By the time my shift is over, I'm exhausted. I stop in the restroom and peer in the mirror. I use one of the brushes to tidy my hair. I want to change into something more attractive, but I don't have many options, which means walking back to my apartment. I leave and wait in the long line outside the building where the interviews are being held. I assume every woman here is hoping for the chance to escape.

When I sit at a table, I'm a little startled to hear the woman interviewing me referred to as a princess.

"Princess?" I ask her after an older woman with a tail walks away.

The woman in question smiles warmly. "Technically, I'm a princess. But not too long ago, I was just like you, living here on Earth and hoping for a better life."

"Oh," I say, flummoxed at that.

"You can just call me Jane," she adds. "Now, let's jump in. The basic requirement for this is a willingness to leave Earth forever to mate with an alien cowboy. You must not have children here. We don't want anyone to leave any children behind. That would be cruel."

"I don't have any family at all," I say quickly. "I'm also more than willing to leave here forever."

I feel her eyes on my arm and realize I forgot about the bruise left from when my brother shook my arm.

"Are you safe here?" she asks softly.

My mind flits to my mother, the only person I ever felt safe with.

"Is any woman really safe on Earth?" I counter.

As soon as I ask that question, Jane's eyes fill with tears. "Not really, no.

Are you ready to leave tonight?"

"Um, yes." I nod so fast that I'm surprised I don't pull a muscle in my neck.

"We schedule these interviews at this hour because I'm familiar with how the shifts run at the factories. I know a lot of women are getting off work now," she explains.

I think about my tiny apartment and how I have no one to tell I'm leaving. "I can leave now," I say without hesitation as a sense of anticipation rises.

HUNTER

I rest my hand on my horse's neck, smoothing over her shimmering fur. "Thank you," I say.

My mount has been with me since I was a boy. Our horses live as long as we do. They are similar to Earth horses but have shimmering fur and thin tails with barbed tips. They can also fly.

Our people's prince glances over to me as he dismounts. "Good work. Are you ready to lead the team to investigate?"

"Of course," I say as if there could be any other answer.

Prince Asher, a longtime friend, claps my shoulder. "Excellent. Talk with Kayden about it and make plans. In the meantime, I hope you'll come tonight to the matching gathering."

My eyes narrow. "Do you think that's wise since I will often be leaving for work?"

Asher studies me for a beat. "Yes, it will give you a reason to come home. Many of our people travel for work."

Our planet has dealt with some unrest lately. For the most part, we are considered one of the most peaceful planets in the galaxy. We are a democracy, but we also have a royal family who leads us. On the other side of our planet, a small group within one of our towns has been protesting the royal family and even kidnapped our new princess. We rescued her, but the aftermath has amped up the stress and concern around their actions. For good reason, of course.

Their dispute is about the royal family succession. I snort to myself whenever I think of it because they want to *be* the royal family.

As a member of the security team for the royal family and one of the spies for our government, I will lead the efforts to infiltrate their group. Working in espionage, I've always been in the background, and I like it that way.

I hold Asher's gaze and slowly nod. "If you think I should, but the women they brought have been here for a while now. If I wanted to mate with one of them, I think I'd know by now."

"Have you even met them all?" Asher asks, a knowing glint in his eyes.

Kayden, another bodyguard and a good friend, approaches. "You have not," he replies. "You've been busy avoiding them."

"If I can," I say dryly.

Kayden's brows arch up. "You must give them a chance."

"You found the infinity pulse," I counter. "I don't know that I will, and I don't think it's worth marrying unless I do."

"Fair point," Kayden agrees. "Yet you won't know unless you meet them all."

"I think you can find the infinity pulse. Give it a chance and come to the gathering tonight," Asher insists.

Although I have my doubts, I can't turn down the invitation. While Asher is a friend, he's also our prince. If he asks me to attend, I shall.

———

When I walk into the gathering that evening, I encounter Princess Jane almost immediately. Her eyes sparkle when she smiles at me.

I dip my head. "Hello, Princess."

She rolls her eyes. "Hunter, you don't need to call me

princess. You know better than I do that we don't stand on ceremony."

I grin. Asher's approaching, and when he stops in front of us, I make a show of bowing to him.

When I straighten, his brows hitch up. "Friend, that's ridiculous, and you know it." He cuffs me lightly on the shoulder.

"We must put on a show. That's the point, isn't it?" I tease.

Jane narrows her eyes. "The point tonight is for you to find a mate. We only have a small group of women from Earth so far. That's not even close to replacing the number of women who died here. The women who have come want to feel safe, so we must welcome them." Jane's gaze sobers.

Several years prior, our planet was hit with an abrupt and destructive space storm during our annual festival to honor women. Many women died. So many that it's threatening our ability to procreate.

Our leadership came up with the idea of bringing women here from Earth since our people have mated with humans for centuries. "I've been to Earth," I say. "It's not a fun place to live."

The leadership on Earth is splintering because they realize they need to do better. They can't cut off intergalactic travel because they're so poor and desperate. They rely on the largesse from other planets for resources and to survive.

We have mated with humans on our planet since cowboys from the American West and France traveled here, making our species strong as a result. Species from most planets mate with other species. Human women aren't our only option, but they are genetically closest to us. We've also discovered that human women become wildly fertile once they come to our planet, and their pregnancies are much shorter. As such, it's the perfect plan to help our people rebuild for future generations.

Some men are thrilled with this, even grumbling that the human women need to get here faster. All the while, Jane insists on screening them. Life on another planet isn't for everyone, even if the planet they leave behind is unpleasant.

Jane nudges me with her elbow. "What's your story?" she asks. "Asher tells me you're not sure infinity pulse exists. He says you like to travel, and that's why you don't want to marry."

I smile at her, winking at Asher as I do. "That's exactly it. I'm a simple man, Jane. It's not complicated. You know that not everyone on our planet experiences the pulse. My parents didn't. They're still married, and I think they're content, but neither one ever met someone with the pulse. They're well past when they could find it."

Our people believe a force called infinity pulse links couples powerfully and deeply. Some couples find it, and some don't. My parents are content. It is also true that I love to travel, as does my father. He raised me with the understanding that since our family's line is involved in espionage here—and on other planets if needed—it may be best that we don't experience infinity pulse.

Jane is drawn away into conversation with one of the human women. Jane herself is human. Asher and I chat a bit about dealing with the uprising in the other town. As we are talking, Kayden approaches with his new mate, Nadine. His tail flicks possessively around her when they stop beside us. He's gaga over her. She is lovely, but I feel nothing but an objective appreciation for Nadine, as well as Jane.

"Have you met Romi?" Jane asks from my side.

Following her gaze, I glance over to see another human woman with long dark hair twisted into a braid atop her head. She's lovely, but it's a purely objective appreciation on my part. I smile and have a polite conversation with her, but it's obvious to Jane there is no infinity pulse for us. She moves along, introducing Romi to others.

I glance at Asher, commenting under my breath. "It's not that I won't mate with any of these women, but I don't feel the pulse. If you'd like, just choose one for me."

Nadine happens to overhear. Her brows furrow with worry, and her mouth presses in a line. "Hunter, you must try."

Kayden glances from Nadine to me. "Sweetheart, you can't

try to experience infinity pulse. It exists, or it doesn't. You know that."

Nadine looks up at him, and I'm surprised sparks don't fly around them; the emotion between them is so intense.

She looks at me apologetically. "He's right. You can't force it, but I want all of my friends who came here from Earth to experience it. Earth is just..." She lets out a little sigh. "It's awful. I want them to have everything that is good here."

Just then, I feel something, an almost electric jolt inside. I glance around, but I don't see anyone. Conversation carries along. A little while later, I feel that same sizzle. This time, it's like a bolt of lightning up my spine. I spin around, searching the room. My eyes lock on a woman. She's standing with Nadine and Kayden. The moment I see her, it feels as if a cord made of fire connects us.

I approach, and Nadine introduces us. I go through the motions of it, but there's static in my brain. All I can think is I need to be alone with this woman.

I stare up at this alien cowboy, feeling breathless. Some qualities about the men on this planet feel so human. I'm aware they descended centuries ago from humans and have mated with us, but it's still a strange feeling. The man's golden eyes study me, and I don't know what to think of this feeling inside. I feel liquid and hot all over.

"Melody," he says.

"Yes?"

"That's a lovely name." He takes a step closer, and I feel a visceral pull in my chest, almost as if a cord connects us and draws tighter with every step.

Heat rises in my cheeks, and my pulse skitters wildly out of control, racing at a breakneck pace.

"Thank you," I whisper breathlessly, a little disconcerted. I swallow and scramble for my composure. "I forgot your name."

"Hunter." He takes another step closer, reaching for one of my hands.

I don't hesitate or pull away, which is unusual because I'm terrified of men. Ever since I was selected to come to this planet to mate with an alien space cowboy, I've been so relieved to escape the desolate, lonely life I'd been leading on Earth. I've been here almost four months now and have started to despair over ever meeting a mate.

Jane keeps telling me that it takes time. It's not that I doubt her, but Nadine found a mate before we even left the planet. I tell myself it's okay, that I don't need to experience the mythical infinity pulse that's supposed to exist here.

With Hunter near, it feels like my body is lit with sparks, and I wonder if it's the infinity pulse. I've never even kissed a man or touched a man beyond being beaten by my own father and later, my brother. I have no idea what to expect. Simply not being abused is more than enough for me.

But this feeling is overwhelming. There's a pleasurable, unfamiliar sensation between my thighs, making me slick and needy.

Hunter's hand is warm, his grip strong and firm. He lifts my hand and turns it over. He dips his head and drops a kiss in the center of my palm. It's a shock to my system and sends a sizzling sensation rippling throughout my body.

I inhale sharply. He takes another step closer. It feels like an electrical force field around us, snapping and crackling. My knees feel wobbly, and that strange sensation between my thighs becomes more powerful.

I lick my lips. "What's happening?"

He takes another step closer. When he brushes against me, my skin feels electric.

"We will mate," he says with slow deliberation, his voice low and gruff. "I will talk to the prince tonight, and we will marry in a week."

After Hunter tells me this, he steps away to ask Jane if he can have a moment alone with me.

Jane holds my gaze, pulling me aside. "Would you like to be alone with Hunter? It's completely your choice."

Although I feel unsettled, churning as though there's a storm inside my body with my emotions stirred up by a fiery wind, all I want is to be alone with Hunter. I'm near desperate for it, and it's confusing for me.

"I do," I say.

Jane's lips curl at the corners. "You feel the pulse."

"Is that what this is?"

She nods slowly. "I can't say for sure, but I believe so. It's like a pull that is so powerful that you cannot turn away from it."

I blink, trying to breathe through the rushing sensation inside.

"I will give you a few minutes alone." She walks me back over to where Hunter waits beside the prince. I study the prince for a moment. He's beautiful, tall with bronze skin and golden eyes, like all the men on this planet.

The moment my eyes shift to Hunter, my belly feels hot and fluttery. That sensation between my thighs begins to throb.

Jane looks at Hunter. "You must respect the guidelines."

Hunter's eyes narrow. "Of course. I know what that means."

My heart is casting out beats so fast I can hardly breathe. He takes my hand and leads me away after Jane tells him where to go. He leads me swiftly down a hallway before he opens the door. His palm is hot on my back.

Once I step into the room, his palm slides down over my bottom, and I gasp. My knees go weak. I feel moisture between my thighs, so much so that I can feel the slickness on my skin.

Hunter's golden gaze holds mine. "We will have to wait a full week."

I lick my lips, swallowing and trying to gather myself. My pulse is racing, and heat blazes like a fast-moving fire through me. "To get married?" I prompt.

"That and to consummate our marriage."

I blink up at him as he takes another step closer. His presence is potent, almost electric. His tail flicks, and I feel the end of it brush my thigh. Jane and my newfound friends from Earth helped me dress for tonight. I'm wearing a simple dress made of a fabric sort of like cotton, but softer. It dips down in a curve over the tops of my breasts and cinches at the waist. The fabric smooths over my hips and flares out to twirl around my ankles. On Earth, I'd worn basically the same thing every day with only a few options. It feels so luxurious here on this planet to have choices.

All this to say, the fabric is thin, and I can feel the brush of his tail through it like a burning strike.

I stare up at him, managing to say, "Oh."

Hunter tilts his head to the side, and I feel the burn of his gaze as it sweeps up and down my body. My nipples tighten to the point of almost aching.

"I'm sure you've heard of the infinity pulse." The low rumble of his voice feels like a caress to my nerves. I almost feel like a cat purring under his attention.

"I have." My voice sounds breathless.

He nods, lifting his hand, his fingers curling as his knuckles trail along my cheekbone. My belly feels liquid. My knees are even more wobbly, and I take a step back, my back colliding with the door as my lips part.

"Have you ever been with a man, human or otherwise?" he asks.

I shake my head, trying to breathe but barely getting any air in.

Heat flares in his eyes at my answer as he takes another step closer. I'm desperate for him even though I'm not exactly sure what I want.

His thumb traces along my jawline before sliding over my bottom lip. His hand dips down, his touch light as air on the side of my neck, and goose bumps rise in its wake. I swallow and hear a subtle whimper coming from my throat as a single fingertip traces along the curve of my neckline before he lightly cups one of my breasts. My back arches into his touch. All I can think is... *more*.

His touch is so subtle as his thumb teases over a nipple

through my dress. He tugs the neckline down just a little. The stretchy fabric gives way, and my breasts plump up over it. I gasp at the feel of his touch on my bare skin. His eyes watch me as my head thumps against the door behind me. I'm near frantic for something, for anything.

As he teases my nipples, he says, "I'm going to kiss you."

A fiery-hot second later, his lips are brushing over mine, and our kiss is a hot shock to my system. It's gentle and so deeply sensual I can hardly bear it. His tongue glides out to tangle with mine. I'm moaning and whimpering into his mouth as he teases my breasts.

I hear myself pleading when he lifts his lips from mine. "I'm going to touch you."

All I can do is nod before his mouth closes over a nipple. When he gives a little suction, the piercing sensation arrows down to that ache between my thighs. My pussy clenches with the need for something, for someone.

He steps back, and I instantly feel bereft, letting out a cry of disappointment.

Hunter's gaze is dark and intent as he reaches for my hand and tugs me away from the door. A few steps later, we reach a desk. His hands smooth down over my hips, gripping before he lifts me and slides my bottom onto the desk. I'm seated right on the edge where my legs are dangling.

He's still watching me as he asks, "May I?"

His hands are on the hem of my dress. I nod because all I want is him, all I want is more.

He drags my dress up to where it rumples around my hips. My knees are already open. The panties that Jane told me to wear are drenched with wetness. He teases his fingers over the wet silk.

When he lifts his eyes to mine, he says, "I'm going to make you find your pleasure. If—"

I cut in, "Please. Hurry."

He hooks his fingers over the edge of my panties and drags

them down, spreading my knees wide. When I look down, I'm a little shocked. I'm pink and glistening, my swollen clit poking out.

When he touches me, I moan, my hips rocking reflexively into his touch.

He reaches for my hand. "Would you like to feel me?"

At my nod, he molds my palm over the front of his breeches. All I want is to feel him inside me. I know instinctively that only Hunter can give me what I want and what I need.

He swiftly opens his breeches, and his shaft springs out. It's thick and long, and the tip glistens with what must be his seed.

"I want to fill you, but I cannot, not yet. But we can do this," he says.

His fingers slide through my slippery folds with one hand as he grips his shaft with the other. I watch as his arousal drips down over me. I've never felt like this. Ever.

"Please," I beg.

Even though I don't know precisely what it is that I need, Hunter gives it to me. His fingers slide inside to fill me and pump in and out. All the while, we watch together as his arousal drips down, making it even more slippery there.

I don't even recognize myself. I want him inside me and his seed filling me. I want to be plump and round with our baby.

I feel a sense of indescribable pleasure tightening inside until he gives me just enough pressure. The pleasure explodes through me, and I cry out. His release drips down.

I'm stunned and almost bewildered at how good I feel as I look up at him. Even though he has just given me more pleasure than I could've ever imagined, I want more as soon as it's over. There's an ache inside, and I want him to fill it.

I take a shaky breath. "I want more."

He dips his head, kissing me as I feel him rubbing the tip of his shaft over me. "There will be more, but not now."

After he pulls away, he helps me tidy myself. He drags my panties up, putting them in place. They're messy from my arousal mingled with his, but I kind of like it. I like the idea of carrying that with me for the evening.

He doesn't leave my side for the rest of that night. With Jane's permission, he walks me back to where I'm staying with the other women from Earth. He kisses me at the gate and whispers, "I'll see you every day until next week when we marry."

Chapter Four

HUNTER

"Remind me why we have to wait a week?" I ask Kayden and Thorne.

Kayden chuckles. "Look who's impatient now," he teases lightly.

"You were impatient to marry Nadine," I point out.

Kayden nods. "Very. I honestly don't know about the waiting period. They say it's tradition and that it is somehow important."

Thorne waggles his brows as he looks over at me. Like me, he's a spy. He will be leaving with our team to go to the other side of the planet in the coming months. We will gather information about those continuing to stir unrest. There's an ongoing trial for those who kidnapped our princess. She is safe, and I predict she will be pregnant again. The infinity pulse binds her and our prince, and they are simply besotted with each other. It's a miracle Asher gets anything done.

"And here you thought it was convenient not to believe in the infinity pulse because you're a spy," Thorne comments.

I roll my eyes. "You've said the same."

"True enough. We'll see if I fall." He glances toward me, flicking his tail mockingly.

"You never do know," I reply. "Did you even go to Princess Jane's gathering the other night?"

Thorne shakes his head. "I did not."

Kayden throws his head back with a hearty laugh. "You can only get away with that so many times."

Thorne's grin is cheeky as he shrugs.

"Now, let's get down to business," Kayden says. "When do we plan to start this operation?" He glances from me to Thorne.

"In a few weeks. And not just because of my wedding," I say. "With the trial, things are a little stirred up over there as it is. Let's wait until they're past the opening arguments on that. Thorne and I have already scouted out options. We think getting temporary jobs at the large warehouse would be best. We can easily blend in there. We thought some others could apply for jobs at the local recycling company. That means they'll travel all over town on a regular basis. They can be there long-term, and we'll travel in and out for the seasonal jobs."

Kayden nods. "Those are good options. Meanwhile, we have another issue with our landing station. Earth is sending a contingent here."

"What?" I ask sharply.

"Asher told me he heard about it from the king. They're aware of our matchmaking plans," Kayden explains.

"How are they even traveling?" Thorne asks.

"I'm assuming in one of their old beater spaceships. They certainly don't have the resources to build new ones, but they haven't traveled much off their planet in decades."

"I don't like this," I say flatly.

"It's a problem for another day," Thorne replies.

"Just keep it on your radar," Kayden adds.

A little while later, I depart the town's governmental offices and walk through the gardens onto the main street. People mostly walk in the downtown area, although we have small hovering vehicles for quicker travel. We use our horses to travel to other towns around the planet. If we need more speed, we go by spaceship.

The central part of town is very well laid out, with various shops concentrated around the primary governmental buildings. I had grown up with my parents right near the downtown area. I think about them as I walk past their home.

I intend to bring Melody to meet them before our wedding, but today, I'm on the way to see Melody. She doesn't know I'm coming, but I'm too impatient for her. It was only last night when I tasted her nectar on my fingers. I need to see her again. The mere thought of her sends a surge of need whipping through me like a storm.

I know from Kayden's bride, Nadine, that Melody works at the local floral shop. It suits her perfectly. I walk briskly down the street, the need inside firing up when I see the sign. I've never had a reason to come in here.

When I walk in, she's waiting on a customer, her smile warm as she hands an elderly man a bouquet. "I'm sure your wife will love them," she says, her cheeks dimpling with her smile.

The customer leaves, the bell jingling above the door as it swings shut behind him. Melody glances up, her cheeks flushing pink as I approach the counter. "Hello." I dip my head slightly when I stop across from her.

She clears her throat, her voice breathy as she replies, "Hello, Hunter."

The mere sound of her voice whips through me, cranking the need more tightly inside. "How are you?"

Melody's pretty eyes blink. Her tongue darts out, sliding across her bottom lip. I want to kiss her.

"I'm well," she finally replies. "Are you allowed to see me?"

I nod. "Of course. I can see you every day, but we must wait to consummate our union until we are bound. Can you take a break?" I ask.

"Of course she can," a feminine voice says.

I glance over to see an older woman smiling. The flush on Melody's cheeks deepens. I want to unwrap her like a present so I can see all of her skin flushed pink. I smile at the woman, who I presume is her boss.

She returns my smile, a knowing glint in her eyes. "Melody isn't used to having breaks, so I usually have to force her to take them," she says with an eye roll. She looks at Melody. "Take your break. You are promised to Hunter. You need to spend some time with him this week. Even though you have the infinity pulse, you should get to know him."

Melody looks at me nervously, and I simply wait. If she doesn't want to leave for a break, I won't press the issue. "Should I leave?" She looks between her boss and me.

"Please do!" the woman says with an airy wave. "This will be a first for her. She usually takes her breaks in the back. Take an entire half an hour, please."

Melody rounds the counter. I reach for her hand, and her fingers lace through mine. At her touch, I can feel the pulse between us tightening and heat streaking up my arm as though flames are leaping across the surface of my skin.

I lead her outside. She looks up at me. "Where are we going?"

"Have you been to see the forest yet?"

She shakes her head. "I've heard it's lovely."

I lead her a few blocks down the street to the arched entrance into the small forest. The trees are silvery, the sun is bright, and there is a soft breeze as we walk along the pebbled pathway. With every step, my pulse races faster and faster, my desire burning hotter and hotter. I have been aching for her, and I need more. Even though I know I must wait, I need to mark her again.

I lead her down a pathway to where I know there are private areas. We stop beside a bench. When she looks up at me, I take a step closer. I savor the sound of her breath drawing in when she feels my hard length against the curve of her belly.

"What if someone sees us?" she whispers.

"No one will see us. Can I kiss you?"

Her lips are already parted. She stares up at me and nods. When she steps a little closer, I can feel the tight press of her nipples against my chest. In a flash, my lips are on hers, and her tongue is teasing with mine. She's making these little whimpering sounds in her throat that drive me wild. Our kiss goes on and on and on. I can't help myself. I tug her dress down, loving the way her breasts plump up over it. Her nipples are deep pink and puckered tightly. I suck one and then the other into my mouth, savoring the way she arches up into my touch.

I slide her skirt up to delve between her thighs. She's not wearing any panties today. I lift my head. "Is this for me?" I tease my fingers into her slippery wet core. Her breath comes out in a little pant as she nods. "Sweetheart, can you turn around for me?"

Obeying with alacrity, she turns, and I draw her dress up around her hips. Her bottom is flushed pink. Without me asking, she bends over the bench, and I look at her pussy, pink and wet. I tease my fingers over her swollen nub, gratified at the way she cries out and her tight little pussy clenches when I sink my fingers inside her. I free my length, cum already rolling down the shaft. I hold it over her bottom, my arousal dripping over her skin. I press some of my seed inside her as I pump my fingers in and out of her.

"Come for me, sweetheart," I tell her.

She cries out when I bury my fingers in her once more with my thumb teasing over her clit. She shudders around me as my release spurts all over her pussy, running down and dripping to the ground underneath us.

It takes me a moment to catch my breath. I turn her around, fingering her from the front before I draw my fingers out and lick her arousal off them. I finally release her dress and hold her close to kiss her so she can taste the mingled flavors of us on her tongue.

I help tidy her clothes. I love knowing that she'll walk around with my seed sticky between her thighs for the rest of the day.

Chapter Five

MELODY

I return to work, feeling almost weak-kneed from the pleasure Hunter wrought on my body. I honestly don't even know how to feel about how good it feels to be with him.

My life on Earth was one of fear with an abusive father and later a brother who also became abusive. Women had next to nothing there. We could work and access online things, mostly because there was no way for the government to cut that off. Kidnappings were common. I'd grown up simply hoping I could keep my head down and no one would notice me. I didn't want to marry, much less ever have children. In fact, I had prayed to be barren.

Now, I crave carrying a baby, quite specifically Hunter's baby. I love it here. The planet is so beautiful. It's a little startling for me to realize that when you have what you need and you're not starving and fighting over resources, so much fear and conflict dissipates.

I glance over at my boss. "Thank you for my lunch break."

She smiles, her eyes twinkling. "Your Hunter is a handsome man. I can feel the burn of the infinity pulse between you."

"Really?" I prompt.

She approaches and places her large hands on my shoulders.

Her skin is beautiful. It's shimmery green and always warm. "My dear, you deserve to feel safe and loved." She waggles her brows. "Hunter is one of the royal family's protectors. You will be safe."

A little anxiety spins in my chest. "I just hope I can"—I let out a little sigh—"satisfy him and be good to him in the way that he needs."

"I see the way he looks at you. You needn't worry. That man is on fire for you, and it will stay that way because of the infinity pulse." She squeezes my shoulders firmly before dropping her hands. "Now, go home. I will see you tomorrow."

As I walk down the street to home, a sense of lightness gusts through me. It's crazy, but this new-to-me planet, where I have no family or anyone I've known until recently, feels more like home than Earth ever did. My mother had been the one bright light in my life. After she died, life felt darker and bleaker.

Here, the air is soft. There's sunshine, rain, trees, flowers, and wildlife. A bright blue bird flies by, flitting about in a tree as I walk past it. I pause to marvel. Someone rides by on one of those horses with sharp tails. Nadine tells me I'll be able to ride one, and I'm so excited.

I turn onto the street leading me to where I'm staying with the other women who came here from Earth. Since I arrived on the first trip, another group has landed. We're still getting to know them. We stay in a house in the royal compound. Princess Jane stops and visits us every day.

Maybe once I feel completely safe, I'll be able to relax. I've been worried that I won't find a mate. I'm more than happy to simply marry a man who won't abuse me. Abuse is all but unheard of here, from what I've been told, because they worship women on this planet. The annual festival they hold here to honor women is what led to the death of so many during a space storm.

When I turn into the gate, I'm aware there's security nearby. Jane assures us we'll be safe, but she was kidnapped by a group on the other side of the planet recently. I try not to think about that much.

A few minutes later, I'm sitting on a comfortable couch holding a glass of lemonade, my new favorite beverage. They cultivate lemons from Earth here. This planet is a hub in the galaxy due to its safety and abundance. Lots of beings travel here from other planets. Before Earth's environment was devastated, they sent seeds here in large quantities, and the people here began cultivating them.

"How was work?" Romi asks as she plunks down across from me, adjusting her dress.

Jane has given us a selection of clothing to choose from. So far, we all favor the soft dresses. It was hard to find pretty clothes on Earth.

I feel myself beginning to blush, and Romi's brows arch. "Did Hunter come to see you?"

I can't help my smile. "He did. He took me to lunch."

"What did you have?" she asks. It's a simple question, but my face burns.

Romi's smile is sly. "I'm guessing you didn't actually eat."

I clear my throat as she laughs softly. "From what I understand, if you have the infinity pulse with someone, they want you all the time." She pauses and shakes her head. "I can't even imagine that. Even the best relationships on Earth were just not abusive."

I nod. "It's hard to feel good about much when you're hungry and poor all the time."

Romi sighs. "There's the green zone and the fake stuff online about fake happiness. As much as I doubt it, I see how the prince is with Jane and now Nadine and Kayden. They're all besotted with each other." Romi falls quiet and studies me for a few beats. "I'm glad you and Hunter have the pulse, but I don't care if I do. I'm happy to mate with someone, have a baby, and be safe." She takes a swallow from her glass. "We have lemonade here. We're safe and clean and dry. I love my job."

"What's your job?" One of the new women walks in. She looks from me to Romi. "I know you work at the flower shop, and Nadine works at the café. Of course, Jane is a princess. But what do you do?"

"I work at the stables. When I was on Earth, I worked at one of the farms, and I'm used to working with animals. Jane told me I didn't have to, but I like it," Romi explains.

One of the new women, Risa, looks concerned, her brow furrowing as she glances between us. "But are there that many options?"

"This isn't like Earth, where there are only a few factories for office work. They have thriving businesses here. When Jane heard I loved flowers, she immediately brought me down there. I heard they have openings at one of the local bookstores and even the intergalactic library," I offer.

Risa's eyes widen. "I would love that. There's hardly anything to read on Earth, but I love to read. Before she passed, my mama had smuggled a batch of books that her mother kept for her. They were passed down through our family. Jane even told me that if I tell her where they are, she'll send someone to try to find them on one of the trips back to Earth."

"Oh, wow," I breathe. "That would be so amazing. I'd love to see them."

"Well, I've already told her where they are. Meanwhile, will we all be attending your wedding?" she asks.

"Of course!" I enthuse. "I'm nervous, though. I need to be ready, and I feel like there's something I should do."

Romi starts to speak just as there's a light knock on the door, and Nadine enters. "Hi, ladies!" She's holding her adorable little baby. "I just thought I'd stop by," she says as she walks into the room. She's so pretty with her honey-blond hair and blue eyes. It's no wonder she met her mate the day she left Earth.

She sits down, and Romi immediately gestures to hold the baby. Nadine happily hands her over. "We were just wondering about the wedding," Romi says as she presses a gentle kiss on the baby's forehead. "Melody is worried about what she should be doing."

"I'm just excited that we actually get to have weddings." Nadine smiles over at me. "You don't have to worry about anything. Helena and her team will plan the whole thing. You and I can meet beforehand for your wedding dress. It will be fitted for you." As she leans back into the couch cushions, I look closely, wondering if her belly already has a curve again.

"Are you pregnant?" I can't help but ask.

Nadine flushes, her hand curving over her belly. "I don't think so."

"How could you be pregnant so quickly?" Jenny, another new arrival from Earth, asks.

"When human women come to this planet, we become very fertile," Nadine says.

Jenny nods, fiddling with the hem of her dress. "Do you want to—" She clears her throat, looking uncomfortable. "Mate?"

My mind flashes to Hunter and the way I feel with him. I cannot wait to grow his baby inside me.

Nadine's cheeks turn a little pink, but she nods. "I promise you, whether you experience the infinity pulse or not, men here are good to women. No one will hurt you. If you experience infinity pulse..." Her eyes slide to mine, and my cheeks burn. "You will want to be with your man as often as you can."

Chapter Six

MELODY

A mere week after Hunter tells me I'll be his mate, I'm standing in a small room with Jane, Nadine, and a seamstress. They're adjusting my dress. I'm nervous but so ready and so impatient. Hunter's mother has just left to go into the area where the ceremony will be held. I met his parents the other day, and they're so kind.

"What do you think?" Jane asks as she turns me to face the mirror.

I don't even know what to think as I stare at myself. The dress is made of cream silk that hugs my hips and twirls around my ankles. Nadine has fixed my hair with white flowers in it. As I look at myself, I remember the dingy mirror we had in the house where I grew up. I remember envying those doing a little better and who could buy from the old stash of things to make themselves pretty.

My life here is a dramatic contrast. Here, I bathe every day so I always feel clean, and wear comfortable clothes. Yet seeing myself looking beautiful with flowers in my hair, I almost start to cry.

Jane gently squeezes my shoulders. "This is your life now, and you are marrying the man you love," she says gently.

My heart starts to beat faster when I think of Hunter. I take a breath to calm myself.

"Are you ready?" Nadine asks from my side, curling her arm around my shoulders.

I turn, looking from her to Jane before I smile. "More than I'll ever be."

The seamstress glances over from where she's putting away her sewing supplies. "You look like a beautiful blushing bride. Now go be one."

A few minutes later, I walk into the large room where they hold these weddings. I attended Nadine's, so I know what to expect, but it still feels overwhelming. There's a rushing sensation inside me. No one is here to give me away because they eschew such a tradition here. Women speak for themselves and pledge themselves freely to whomever they choose.

I choose Hunter.

I'm lost in the blur of his golden eyes throughout the ceremony as he pledges to protect me, to honor me, to cherish me, and to love me into infinity.

Somehow, I manage to repeat the words back to him. I'm finally grounded when his lips meet mine to seal our vows with a kiss. Although Hunter's touch sends my pulse into the stratosphere, I feel safe with him. When he's close, I feel even safer.

He lifts his head, his eyes locking on mine. "I love you," he whispers.

I can't even speak, but I press my palm to his heart, and he smiles. We are swept into the celebration after this. The food is plentiful, and the drinks flow. It is lovely to be celebrated in such a way, yet I am so impatient to be alone with Hunter.

I know we have our own house waiting for us and a week all to ourselves. At one point, I look up at him and can't help but ask, "When are we allowed to go home?"

Chapter Seven

HUNTER

When are we allowed to go home?

"Now," I say in response to Melody's question.

Time has crawled by since I met her, and I knew beyond any doubt that she is mine and will be into infinity. Since then, all I have wanted is to be with her. In honesty, I'm a little concerned about how I'm going to even work after a week of pleasure with her. But the prince and Kayden seem to manage it, so I'm banking that I can as well.

I catch the prince's eyes. He knows without me saying anything that I would like to depart. I'm sure he can understand after his own wedding. He stands, tapping his glass with a fork. The room quiets.

"The newlyweds are off. Let us cheer them and wish them nothing but love," he announces.

When we leave, Melody's hand is warm in mine. The walk to our new home isn't far. Once we close the gates in our garden, I squeeze her hand a little tighter. I'm beyond impatient. I have been for the entire week. As soon as we are in the house, I press her against the door and begin kissing her.

She opens for me so readily as we stumble toward the kitchen. I lift her onto the counter and spread her knees wide.

She's flushed pink all over, and I dip my head to kiss her again, long and slow.

"You're mine now," I rasp when I lift my head.

Melody's lips curl in a soft smile. "As you are mine," she whispers in return, desire flashing in her eyes.

I want to take this slow, to savor every second of it. But I have been waiting for what feels like forever. I bring my lips to hers again. Our kiss is a lazy tangle of tongues. I push her knees apart before I finally break free of her sweet mouth to lean down and trail hot, open-mouthed kisses along the insides of her thighs.

She's trembling when I finally bring my mouth to her sex. She cries out, and I feel the clench of her channel when I sink two fingers inside. Her taste is salty and sweet. I breathe her in as I tease her, driving myself to distraction as much as her. I lift my head to watch as I fuck her with my fingers.

Her skin is flushed, her lips parted as she pants. I finally give her the pleasure I know she needs, burying my fingers deeply just as I bring my mouth to her and lightly suck on her clit. She shudders, clamping down around my fingers. I ride it out with her until her trembling slows.

When I straighten, I bring my mouth to hers, kissing her and giving her a taste of her own arousal. When I draw back, it's all I can do not to rip her dress off and take her right here. The only thing holding me back is that I want to feel all of her bare skin against me.

"Are you ready?" I ask against her mouth.

I catch her answer with another kiss when she whispers, "Yes."

Chapter Eight

MELODY

Are you ready?

I feel as if I'm tumbling into this fire that Hunter kindles higher and higher with every touch, with every kiss. He draws away from my mouth, and for a moment, I feel bereft, wanting to drag him back to me. He lifts me in his arms, holding me against his chest in his strong embrace.

I feel so protected with him, so safe. The feeling is intoxicating because I've never experienced it. I take in glimpses of our home as he strides through the living room area with windows looking out over gardens and the blue mist of the mountains in the distance. A big couch with a brightly colored rug is on the floor. Everything feels open and airy and inviting.

He walks through a small arch and down a short hallway that leads to another door. He's holding me securely as he opens it, saying, "This is our bedroom."

He lowers me to the floor. I don't even remember taking my silk slippers off, but I must've at some point. I follow his lead as he begins to undress swiftly. We leave a trail of clothes behind us, reaching for each other in between for quick touches, kisses, and more.

When my dress pools at my feet, and I'm standing at the

foot of our bed, Hunter stops me. I take a moment to absorb the sight of him. He is a stunning, powerful being. The light plays over his shimmery bronze skin. When his tail flicks, my entire body feels electrified.

I try to breathe, but I can barely manage it. He asks again, "Are you ready?"

"Yes," I whisper.

This feels more right than anything I could've imagined. All I want is to be joined with him. What follows is second after second, heartbeat after heartbeat, of sensation. My nerve endings feel alive and sparkling.

Our kisses go on and on in a tangle of lips, teeth, and tongues. His hands map my body, his mouth leaving blazing trails of sparks everywhere he touches. My belly trembles when he smooths a calloused palm over it. He drops hot kisses on my thighs, and goose bumps rise on my skin as I shiver with fiery anticipation.

His fingers tease me again. I whimper at the feel of his warm skin as he comes over me. His thick shaft is swollen with need for me, cum rolling out the tip and dripping onto me. And then, finally, *finally*, his weight rests over me.

His hands brush my tangled hair away from my face as he asks yet again, "Are you ready?"

The answer is a foregone conclusion as I whisper, "Yes."

I feel his thick crown nestle against the very heart of me. He fills me in a slow glide. The burning sensation is brief and intense, but it passes.

He holds still, asking if I'm okay, distracting me with his mouth and his words. "I love you. You are mine."

Once again, I experience a jolt of knowing, of awareness in his golden gaze, echoing mine. He seats himself deeply, and I savor the feel of him filling me again and again until he reaches between us. He teases over the center of my pleasure, and it bursts through me in a ray. I feel sparks scattering through me as

I cry his name and shudder and feel the heat of his release filling me inside.

He rolls us over, holding me against him. "I love the way you feel," I rasp.

After we rest for a few moments, he lifts me and carries me into our bathroom. This is the first time I'm even able to see it. Like the rest of the house, it is also bright and open with the light from the setting sun falling through the windows. We shower together. I feel so cared for when he helps towel me off afterward. We dress in robes before he takes me on a small tour of our house.

We have our own bedroom and bathroom. The bed is big with pillows and brightly colored sheets. A door leads out to our garden. I'm still adjusting to the flowers and trees here. It's so different from Earth, where all you see are the old remnants of forest and dead trees.

Our private suite is on one side of the home, with the living room and kitchen in the middle and another hallway with more bedrooms on the other side. We even have a guest suite if we ever have visitors.

"I love it." I look up at Hunter when we're back in the kitchen.

He smiles down at me, his eyes warm. "This is your home forever." His gaze sobers after a moment. "Are you glad you're here?"

"Absolutely," I say, a sense of joy rising inside. "I love it here, and I love you."

He kisses me again before stepping back and asking, "Are you hungry?"

"I am because I was too nervous to eat much after our wedding," I tell him.

Chapter Nine

MELODY

Over the following week, I lose myself, or maybe find myself, in my time with Hunter. Beyond simply getting to know him and savoring the pleasure of being with him intimately, I learn so much about my new home and planet.

I'm surprised to discover the prince and princess live essentially like the rest of us. I had expected to be in a less luxurious home than theirs.

When I comment to Hunter, "This is so much like Princess Jane's place," his lips twitch at the corners as he nods.

"Yes. Very much so. They have larger grounds and additional security, but as our leaders, they have been beloved for centuries because they are like all of us. There is enough for everyone here."

Our house is a little smaller than Jane and Asher's, but it's so nice, and we have food delivered for the week. Hunter explains all couples can avail themselves of this. Some don't choose to, but they can. I'm still getting used to all the fruits and vegetables available here. We have a large garden on our grounds.

Hunter tells me, "You can garden to your heart's content. If it's not your thing, we can hire someone to manage it, but I thought I'd ask. I enjoy it when I'm not working, but sometimes I have to travel."

"I know I'll love it," I enthuse as I look at the flowers and select fruits for breakfast.

About halfway through our week alone, I study him for a moment. "How often will you be traveling?"

I already know from Jane and Nadine that the men who are part of the royal family's security contingent will travel whenever the prince needs them around the planet. I also know Hunter's job is a little different because he's a spy.

He holds my gaze, rotating his hand back and forth as he replies, "It depends on what's happening. After this time with you, I will need to go to the other side of the planet to scout out the town where those are protesting the line of succession." He rolls his eyes.

"I heard about that, that they kidnapped Jane. I don't understand. Everything here is so nice."

Hunter nods. "It is. But history everywhere tells us there are always people who want power for power's sake. And they are those kinds of people. Over the centuries here on our planet, even though we're a democracy, the royal family is a figurehead, but they get elected. There's a line of succession. After we lost so many women, Asher traveled to Earth to find a bride. He had not experienced the infinity pulse with anyone. He needed to see if that was a possibility. We also need women."

His eyes darken as he holds my gaze, and my body reacts instantly. I feel almost as if I'm primed for him and him alone. "I'm not glad that your planet lost so many women, but I'm glad you came to Earth and that I'm here now. With you."

His eyes flicker with fire as he steps close to kiss me. After a moment, he lifts his head. I can't help but ask, "Do we need to worry about what's happening in the other town?"

He shrugs. "Yes and no. Every few years, they raise more of a ruckus. The funny thing is they claim they don't believe in the royal family, yet what they want is to *be* the royal family." He shakes his head slightly. "There are currently trials ongoing for those involved in the princess's kidnapping. That's keeping people stirred up in that town."

"I've heard rumors that those men are trying to do what they did on Earth, to take away rights from women and take things away from people, keeping resources only for those in power. That makes me nervous," I say.

Hunter nods and reaches for my hand. "That is accurate, but you don't need to worry. It's one town and one small group of people. Our planet is one of the most abundant in the galaxy. No one wants to lose what we have. We take care of each other and everyone here," he assures me.

"Okay," I say.

As we stand there, I'm once again ensnared in his golden gaze. My pulse races as liquid need spins through my veins. He drops my hand and slides his palm around my waist, down over my bottom, and pulls me flush against him. I feel the hard, hot length of him against my belly.

"I want you. Now," he rasps.

My breath is shallow, and my lips part as he palms my cheek with his other hand, sliding his thumb across my bottom lip. A fiery second ticks by before he bends low and claims my mouth. We're in the garden, out in the open.

Like always. I'm nearly desperate for him. I can't get enough. I drag my hand over his length between us. I know what I want. When we break apart, I take a step back to the bench behind me. "Stay right there."

The boldness I experience with Hunter is something I never would've imagined before. On Earth, all I wanted was to hide. I didn't want any man to notice me. I couldn't have imagined commanding a man when I wanted something. With Hunter, I feel open and safe.

I swiftly undo his breeches, leaning forward to slide my tongue across the tip of his length, where it glistens with his arousal. I love the salty tang of it. I push his pants down around his hips before I drag my tongue along the bottom of his shaft, angling my head to the side and watching his gaze darken. His fingers tighten in my hair when I suck him into my mouth. He's shown me what he likes, which empowers me. He loves it when I curl my palm around his length and slide it up and down, drawing his seed from him. I tease him again and again as I suck him in.

"Melody," he growls. I draw back, releasing him with a pop as I look up at him. "I need to be inside you."

"Now?" I bite my lip as I stare up at him, wanting to drive him just a little bit closer to the edge as I lean down and swipe up another drop of cum with my tongue.

"Yes, now," he rasps.

I don't hesitate to stand from the bench and turn around. I'm wearing a dress, as I do almost every day. Beyond the comfort, they make it easy to find pleasure with him.

I kneel on the bench as he slides my dress up over my bottom. His fingers tease between my thighs, and I cry out, pushing back. "Hurry," I plead.

Seconds later, I feel the thick press of him at my entrance, and he fills me in a swift thrust. I cry out at the delicious stretch. I'm impatient, chasing my release already. I love that he never makes me wait for it. Sometimes he draws it out a little bit. He's shown me how, if I wait, my release can be more powerful. But sometimes, like now, I know I need it right away. I need the fast, fiery release.

As he fills me in slow, deep pumps, he reaches around, teasing over my swollen button of need. It's slippery and hard.

Just when I think I can't take it anymore, he gives me just the right amount of pressure, and my climax ricochets through my body as his name follows in a shuddering breath.

Chapter Ten

HUNTER

I look down at Melody's bottom. Her skin flushes rosy pink as I slide in and out of her dripping wet pussy. I'm barely clinging to my control. When she comes, the core of her rippling around my length, I listen to the sound of my name in her throaty voice. I draw back once more, sinking in as my release slams through me in a hot sizzle of lightning.

Until her, until Melody, until experiencing the pulse with her, I wouldn't have imagined how much it would matter to me to mark her with my seed, to fill her, to impatiently wait to know that she's carrying our baby. I curl around her as I catch my breath.

A moment later, I reluctantly withdraw from her, looking down to see the sticky evidence of our intimacy on her thighs. The flame of need starts burning again.

It amazes me I can want her so swiftly. At the sight of her bent over, bared to me, my cock twitches even though I have just found my release. I lift her in my arms and sit on the bench with her on my lap. She presses kisses on the side of my neck as I lazily undo the buttons on her dress until it falls open. I drag it out of the way so she's naked in my lap. I tease her breasts, sucking a nipple into my mouth, gratified when she cries out and arches up into me. Her thighs fall open when I slide my palm over her belly and dip between them. She's wet from the mingling of our arousal.

"Again?" I ask as I catch her mouth with a kiss.

I love how I feel the curve of her smile against my lips when she nods. Her cheeks are pink when I lift my head. "Is it ever enough?" she asks.

"I don't know," I answer honestly.

Without prompting, she straddles me.

"Watch," I say as I fist my length and notch it at her entrance. Her clit is hard and poking out. We watch together as I slide into her, and she sheaths me in her clenching core. Only moments later, she's calling my name, coming all over my cock as I fill her once more.

————

On the last morning of our week alone, I sit across from her in our kitchen. Melody has her feet hooked around the legs of a stool. She's tracing idle patterns on the counter with her fingertip as she looks out the window. The light from our planet's sun angles through, casting a golden glow across the room and leaving shimmering streaks of gold in her hair.

My chest tightens, and it feels as if a fist is clenching my heart tightly. Now that I'm experiencing the infinity pulse, my old cynicism about it is completely gone. I feel sad for anyone who doesn't get to experience it.

Yet it's terrifying. Because I must leave her for work, for the calling I have carried within me my entire life. I have faith I will be safe, but I know I will miss her deeply, even for my brief travels away from her.

"We need to talk about my work," I say.

Melody takes a swallow from her favorite morning drink, a sweet tea. Her lashes lift, her pretty eyes locking with mine. "I know you must travel. It's part of your job, your life. Jane has already told me about that. Just like Asher and Kayden and any of the men who work to protect the royal family."

I nod and reach for her hand across the counter. "You know I'm a spy."

Melody nods. "I do. How much can you tell me about your work?"

"Tomorrow, I'll need to go. I'm leading a group that will be monitoring in the town where the protests started and where they took Jane when they kidnapped her."

"Will you be safe?" Her brow wrinkles with her question.

"I will," I assure her. "Our people are not violent. Even those who are doing dangerous things."

"But they kidnapped Princess Jane, and they tried to keep some of the men, like Kayden and the others," she interjects.

"I know. They did, but they didn't hurt them, and they didn't hurt Jane. I'll be safe. When I'm gone, protectors will always watch over our property and you. You are under that protection because I'm part of the royal team. The whole town is here."

Melody blinks, and I can see the worry chasing through her gaze. "How long will you be gone?"

Chapter Eleven

MELODY

"He couldn't tell me how long he'll be gone," I say to Jane and Nadine. "He said it wouldn't be more than a week at a time, though."

"He'll be safe," Jane says with more confidence than I feel.

"That's what he said, but I worry."

Just then, Romi walks into the room with Risa, Jenny, and Hannah, all from the newer group that recently arrived from Earth.

"Hi," Jane says warmly as she stands to greet them, grasping each woman by the hands.

I haven't actually met Hannah yet because she arrived while I was enjoying my week alone with Hunter. Jane glances from me to Nadine as she gestures in an arc, saying, "This is Nadine and Melody. Melody is just back from her week with her new mate."

Romi sits down beside me, curling her arm around my shoulders and giving me a squeeze. I'm still adjusting to having friends like this. The bond I feel with the women who came here with me is powerful. On Earth, life didn't leave much room for friendship. It was simply a scramble to stay alive. I had friends when I was younger, but depending on where we ended up working and what happened to our families, we couldn't see each other often.

It's so different here. Kindness and safety make it much easier to make friends and form those bonds on this planet.

"How was your week?" Romi asks before leaning forward to pour herself a glass of lemonade.

As she does frequently, Jane has invited us over. The table encircled by the couch has an array of snacks and drinks.

I feel my cheeks getting hot as I smile. "It was amazing." I look around, adding, "Honestly, it's better than I could've imagined. Hunter is so good to me."

Nadine's eyes twinkle with warmth. "I'm so glad. I'm sure you're already pregnant," she says.

"After just a week? Do you really think so?" Hannah asks.

"It's hard to believe or imagine, but women from Earth become much more fertile once we're on this planet," Jane chimes in. "The scientists here think it's something to do with the environment. They also believe the strain of living on Earth affects our fertility there. It's highly likely that Melody is already pregnant."

"I won't know until I miss my monthly time," I say. "Now, we wait. Hunter is traveling for work this week, and I'm so impatient for him to be back. "

"Asher's and his security team are traveling the planet and visiting all the different towns. I will join him for part of the journey later this week. It's kind of funny." Jane's lips curl in a smile when she pauses. "Asher told me I have to make sure to post about it on GalaxyCosmo. I've forgotten all about that since I've been here. It's such a big deal on Earth because it's all they have for news and information. Since I've been living here, actual life is so much more interesting. I don't even wonder what anybody's doing online." She rolls her eyes a little. "Asher tells me it's important. I can't help but think maybe I should look up my ex-fiancé, the one who screwed around with my best friend. They never did post if they were officially a couple when I was still on Earth."

"I rarely had access to a phone when I was on Earth because I didn't have a regular office job," I tell them.

"We'll get you one here if you want," Jane offers. "Those phones were about the only thing that the government on Earth made sure we had."

"Probably because that was the only way we got some of the most basic supplies," Risa says. "I still can't believe I'm here. Everything is so nice and beautiful. Honestly—" She looks toward me. "I'm glad you mated with someone where you can experience this pulse thing I keep hearing about, but I just want to be safe. I don't care about anything else."

I contemplate my week with Hunter, reflecting on how I felt before meeting him. "I totally understand," I tell her, "but if you meet someone and experience the pulse, I promise it will feel amazing."

Our conversation moves along. Jane plans to host another gathering for the women from Earth to meet possible mates, and we answer an array of questions from the new arrivals.

"Where did you meet Hunter?" Risa asks.

"At one of those gatherings," I reply, thinking back to that night and how quickly I recognized our connection.

"We should talk about work options," Jane says. "Nadine works at the local coffee shop and loves it."

"And I work at the floral shop across the street from the café and love it. Romi works out at the stables, and you love your job too, right?" I look toward Romi.

Romi nods vigorously. Her dark hair is pulled up in a ponytail and bounces with the motion. "I worked at the stables on Earth as well. Obviously, it's very different here. The horses here are amazing. Speaking of—" She glances toward me. "One of the men I work with told me that when Hunter is back, he'll bring you out to ride."

"Nadine has started a support group too," Jane adds. "It's a great opportunity for support and to learn what it's like to live here because it is so very different from Earth."

As I look around the group, it strikes me how quickly I have adjusted to living here. Oh, there's no doubt I'm still overwhelmed with my new life and with so many changes in such a short time. I suppose I'll always carry anxiety and fears, and even scars, from growing up the way I did. It's easier to become accustomed to a new life when the place is such a vast improvement. The new women who arrived have the shell-shocked expression I must've had when I got here. Jenny exclaims over the taste of the lemonade while Hannah marvels at the selection of fruit.

Out of nowhere, a giggle slips out of me, and Romi slides her gaze to mind, asking, "What's so funny?"

"It's just crazy. We've been here for months, and I still can't believe it. It's almost funny." I shrug.

Nadine smiles between us. "I still get happy nervous moments. Life here is something truly beyond what we could've imagined on Earth," she says.

———

The following day, I'm at work. My boss has sent me to the farm where we grow our flowers. We have a small garden immediately behind the florist shop, but there's a much bigger one a few blocks away.

I'm walking down the street when I hear the whooshing sound in the air from what I recognize as the sound of the horses. I glance over to see a beautiful small one, gliding low across the ground. She's so pretty, shimmering almost pink. As she goes by, I could swear she catches my eye, a glint of warmth in her dark eye.

"But that's crazy," I say to myself.

Instinctively, I smooth my hand over my belly. I'm not sure if I'm pregnant yet, but I hope I am. On Earth, the last thing I wanted was to be pregnant. My goal on Earth had been to end my family's lineage with me. I'd hoped my brother never even found someone to mate with. It feels so different here. I cannot wait to have a baby and create a family with Hunter.

I could swear there's a tingling sensation inside me as if a life is burgeoning. I reach the flower farm and jingle the little bell on the gate. The elderly orc, the primary gardener, lifts his head and smiles at me.

"Melody, hello, my dear," he says as he approaches.

My eyes rise up and up and up as I tilt my head back. He's tall, as all orcs tend to be. "Hi, Harold," I say. "I'm here to gather some flowers for the shop."

He dips his chin, gesturing with his large hand toward a row of buckets. "I already have them ready for you."

"Did she call ahead?" I ask.

He waggles his brows as his mouth kicks into a half smile. "Of course, she did. I'll help you load them up."

I eye the row of buckets of flowers. "That would be very helpful," I say.

I could load them myself, but I know Harold likes to do it. He has a hovercraft that he keeps on-site. It's programmed to carry me right back to the floral shop and come back to him on its own. In short order, he has everything loaded on the platform on the back for me. He gallantly gestures, swinging his arms. "Your chariot awaits," he teases.

As I stop beside him, I smile up at him. "Thank you for being so kind to me, Harold."

"Melody, why would I be anything other than kind? I might not be from this planet either, but I came here for a reason. It is safe and peaceful. I'm glad you're here as well," he says, his eyes warm.

Tears sting the backs of my eyes. I don't know if I'll ever get used to the genuine kindness here. But then, I suppose it's easier for people to be kind when they know they are cared for and matter.

Harold helps me up into the hovercraft, and I thank him again before hovering my way back to the floral shop. The rest of the day passes quickly as we're very busy. A local family is hosting a gathering to celebrate the grandparents, who have been married for seventy years. That's a shocking number to me, if only because, on Earth, most people don't even live past fifty. In contrast, this planet is renowned for the health of its people and the medical care here.

One of the granddaughters, who's not much younger than me, stops by the store to pick up the flowers they've ordered. "Melody!" she exclaims as her gaze sweeps across the table where the flowers are all waiting to be picked up. "These look beautiful!"

"Thank you, Verbena," I say. "I am honestly amazed at how long your grandparents have been married and wanted to honor their union. Coming from Earth, it's just, well, extremely unusual for something like this to happen."

She nods in understanding. "That's what I hear. My grandparents have the infinity pulse, and—" Her lips quirk at the corners with her smile. "They just love each other so much. I hope you and Hunter find the same happiness. I'm so glad you're married."

My heart feels like hands clapping with joy when it pounds in response. "I hope so too. No matter what, I feel lucky to have found Hunter, and I hope we have a family."

I help her load the flowers on the back of her hovercraft and assure her I will see her that evening for the celebration. Princess Jane has already arranged for us all to attend, including the new women. She described it as "An excellent opportunity for them to meet new people."

Chapter Twelve

MELODY

When I return home after work, I instantly miss Hunter when I walk inside. It's disconcerting, but his absence is a physical experience for me. My heart feels as if something is tugging on it. Nadine has explained to me that, because of the infinity pulse bonding us, there will be times I can experience a physical pull toward wherever Hunter is located, even if it's on the other side of the planet. She has experienced that whenever Kayden travels.

I place my palm above my heart, feeling comforted to miss him and feel that pull. It reminds me of all we share. I pause for a moment and spin in a slow circle. I imagine I will marvel at having a house like this for the rest of my life.

My parents had a small home on Earth, and I'd felt lucky. Just as I had when I got my own apartment after I got my job. It might've been dingy and in a crowded building and a single small room, but it had been mine.

The home I share with Hunter here feels beyond luxurious. I like that the people on this planet focus on simplicity. Hunter and I have space for us and the family we will create, and that's enough. Beyond our bedroom are two other bedrooms for the children I hope will come soon. Our pretty garden feels like almost too much extravagance to enjoy outside.

My little communicator beeps, and I hear Nadine's voice coming through. "I'll meet you at your gate and walk with you to the celebration if you'd like."

I tap the communicator, replying, "Of course! I'm getting changed right now. I'll see you soon."

I hurry into our bedroom and quickly take a shower. I love how the sunlight streams through the windows above the shower. Most of us reached a point on Earth where we tried to avoid the sun because it was so hot and dry there. Here, I love that I can enjoy it. The light is softer, and it makes everything sparkle.

I'm refreshed and feel ready for the night after my shower. The dress I selected tonight is a bright blue color that Hunter tells me brings out my eyes. I wish he were here. I know he'll be home soon, but the ache of missing him is visceral.

———

Romi stands at my side at the gathering, holding a glass of a fizzy drink they make here. I understand it's like alcohol, which was extremely rare on Earth. I'm abstaining from anything like that right now, in case I'm pregnant.

She takes a swallow and lets out a happy little sigh. "This stuff is so good." She smiles at me, her eyes bright. "I'm nervous," she blurts out.

"You're nervous?" I'm surprised at this. Romi comes across as bold and confident to me.

She sets her glass down on the table beside us and smooths her hands over the front of her dress. "Yes. I'm kind of a tomboy. I'm not as beautiful as you, Jane, and Nadine."

I turn to face my friend, reaching for her hands and squeezing them before I release them. "Romi, you're stunning. To me, you're like a powerful goddess."

She is quite a bit taller than me. I look up at her, studying her angled cheekbones, her straight nose with her dark brows, and her glossy dark hair. Romi has a fierceness to her that originally intimidated me, but now I know her to be kind and deeply protective of those she cares about.

Uncertainty flickers in her eyes. "I don't need to experience the infinity pulse." She waves a hand dismissively. "I just want to mate with someone. I worry if I don't find someone soon that I won't be able to stay here."

"Romi, Jane assures us that will never happen. You're going to find someone. According to Jane, it's going to take years before the population recovers from the women they lost. You're safe here. You train and care for the flying horses, and I'm still scared to ride one."

Romi's smile is warm. "When Hunter's back, I'll be there for your first lesson, I promise."

As I glance around, I notice that multiple men have their eyes on her. I know she will find the right mate.

Nadine approaches, stopping beside us when Kayden steps away to confer with another man about something. "You both look amazing tonight," she says warmly.

"How's the baby?" I ask.

Nadine's lips curl in a soft smile. "Perfect."

"Are you going to get pregnant again right away?" Romi teases as she nudges Nadine playfully with her elbow.

When Nadine's cheeks turn pink, Romi's mouth drops open in faux surprise. "I'm shocked. You and Kayden can't even keep your eyes off each other, much less your hands," she teases.

Nadine presses her lips to keep from smiling. "I'm not pregnant again. Yet." She slides me a look. "And we're still waiting for you to announce your pregnancy."

Instinctively, I slide my hand over my belly. Although it feels mostly flat, I could swear it's slightly rounder. "I hope to find out soon, but I'm waiting."

"Do you miss Hunter?" Nadine asks.

"So much," I say earnestly, feeling the words in my heart.

Chapter Thirteen

HUNTER

"They think they arrested all of us, but they didn't," a man named Marco tells me.

I nod. "We've heard about the protests. That's why I traveled here. We want to be part of it if we can, but we can't live here all the time. We have families and work," I explain.

"Understood," he says.

"How many weren't caught? There's a lot of men on trial," I point out.

"Those men were part of the planning for the kidnapping. Most of them have been arrested." He rolls his eyes. "I told them that was a risky operation, but they were arrogant and thought too much of themselves." He nods sagely, almost to himself.

I nod along with him and keep the conversation rolling while this man tells me way more information than he ever should. I learned there are still people involved in the original operation to kidnap Princess Jane who haven't been identified and arrested. They were part of the planning, but they weren't part of the operation to kidnap her, so they've avoided detection so far.

The spies from our team who have come with me have also easily integrated into this group. We meet our new friends at the local watering house. A bit of drink loosens tongues. We assure them we will continue to support their messages of protest in our town and anywhere we travel.

A week later, the group of spies reconvenes about halfway between this town and our planet's capital, where we live, to check in. I glance among the group, asking, "Thoughts?"

Thorne, one of my close friends and a loyal team member, speaks first. "Nothing we didn't expect. We'll need to figure out how to arrest the others involved in the kidnapping without tipping off who we are."

"Agree," I say. "I think perhaps we talk with Princess Jane if Asher consents. Although the operation took place in the darkness, perhaps she can speak to any names she may have heard."

Raven chimes in, "When we interviewed her initially, she mentioned several other men whose voices she heard that night. That may be enough. We can ask those handling the current trials to do fresh interviews with those being held. They may turn on the others."

"They're facing long sentences," I point out. "Let's do both. Meanwhile, we'll return home and discuss visiting other towns in another week. The prince is touring the planet as he does annually. He'll be bringing Princess Jane with him for some of the visits. It's a good time for us to accompany them, along with the rest of the security detail."

We begin our flight home. Whenever we do missions like this, which isn't too often, we disguise ourselves and use horses from the training herd. Aside from our personal horses, we have a fleet for the security detail. We provide security to the royal family and the governmental buildings, along with spying when necessary.

As we take flight, I feel the pull of the infinity pulse get stronger. I began missing Melody from the moment we left. I accept this feeling will be part of my life whenever I have to travel away from her. Although I'd heard experiencing the pulse involves a physical sensation regardless of the distance, it still surprises me. It feels as if there is a cord that connects us no matter the distance between us.

As I get closer to my home and to her, the sensation becomes more powerful. I cannot wait to be with her again. Although our horses fly swiftly, it still takes time to get from one side of the planet to the other. I land with our contingent at the stables on the outskirts of town.

Romi works here and comes over to help. When I glance toward Thorne, I realize this is the first time he has seen her. His eyes narrow as he appraises her. She doesn't notice him at first, but when I see her turn in his direction, their eyes lock.

I think to myself, that maybe, just maybe, Thorne has met his match. He's broody and tends to be distant with most women. He lost his mother when he was young.

Romi blinks before she turns to me. "Glad you're back safe and sound," she says. "Melody has missed you."

My lips instantly curl. "As I have her. Do you need me to stay while you put my mount away?"

Romi shakes her head quickly. "Of course not. It's my job." She smiles, sliding her hand down the shimmery silver-black fur of my mount. "He's one of my favorites."

"Thank you." I flick a glance at Thorne, who all but glowers at me. "Thorne is a good man," I offer. "He would make a good mate. Just ignore it if he's a grump with you."

Romi's cheeks pinken when she looks over toward Thorne for a few seconds before bringing her attention back to me. "A grump, you say?" She lifts her chin slightly.

I chuckle. "Yes. I have no doubt you can handle him. After all, you train these horses when they're wild." I dip my head. "Thank you again."

As I stride past Thorne a moment later, I say, "Watch yourself."

"What do you mean?" he calls to my back.

"You'll figure it out," I call in return.

I break into a run as I turn through the gates to our small

property. Moments later, I burst through the door, calling, "Melody!"

She turns from where she is in the kitchen, a smile unfurling across her face. My heart kicks so hard in my chest it hurts. I stop abruptly, simply taking a moment to absorb the vision of her. Her hair is down, silky and pretty around her shoulders. Her eyes are wide and her cheeks pink. She's wearing a sundress.

I watch the flush spread down her neck and across her chest. The collar of her dress dips low over her breasts. I could swear they're fuller than they were the last time I saw her. Awareness sizzles in my body, and I know she's carrying our baby.

I stop in front of her, reaching for her hands. Her touch instantly grounds me, soothing the ache of missing her.

"I've missed you," she says. She tugs one hand free, placing her palm over my heart as she takes a step closer.

My heart lurches toward her, recognizing the one who holds it. "As I've missed you," I say.

I slip my arm around her waist. Although our connection goes far beyond desire, this desire is part of what binds us together. At this moment, my sheer need for her is nearly overwhelming.

I slide my palm down over the sweet curve of her bottom, taking one more step until we are flush together. I know she can feel the swell of my arousal against her low belly.

"You are with child," I say, my lips brushing against hers as I bend low.

"I think so," she whispers in return.

"I need you."

"I'm yours." Her words form against my lips.

I claim her mouth with a kiss, loving how she opens for me instantly, her tongue boldly twining with mine as my hand tangles in her hair. The following moments are a fumbled rush. I tug her dress down over her breasts, bending low to give a hard suck on one nipple as I tease the other with my thumb.

She cries out, arching into my touch and another shot of

blood arrows to my cock. I savor every touch, the sweet scent of her, the feel of her curves, her silky soft skin, and every little sound she makes.

Near frantic with my need for her, I lift my head, nudging her backward into the kitchen toward the counter. I spin her around and drag her dress up over her hips, letting out a little growl of satisfaction at the sight of her bottom. Her skin is stained pink with the flush of her passion.

I nudge her thighs apart with my knee, glancing down as I smooth a hand over her spine and she stretches out on the counter. Our week together gave us time to get to know each other. I know I will learn her thoroughly over the years we share.

I'm gratified she knows already that I love to take her from behind like this sometimes. I glance down to see her pussy pink and glistening, her arousal smeared on the insides of her thighs. She's dripping wet.

"All for me?" I murmur as I bend over and nip lightly at her ear.

She shivers under my touch, pressing her bottom back into me as she gasps. "Yes, I missed you so much."

With desperate need pounding like a fist inside my body, I swiftly reach between us, freeing my shaft from my breeches and shoving them down around my hips, just enough to grip my length. I tease the thick head between her folds, getting it slippery. Her arousal mingles with the cum already rolling out of my tip, dripping over her as I draw back slightly and notch myself at her entrance.

"Are you ready?" I ask, barely able to hold back my release.

She presses her hips back, saying, "Hurry, please, Hunter..."

I fill her in a swift surge, pumping deeply.

I hold her hip with one hand and reach around to tease over her plump clit. She's already chasing her release. I feel her body quickening, and her hips keep rocking back to meet each thrust as I fill her again and again.

"Come for me, sweetheart," I rasp.

Just like that, she shudders, her pussy clamping down as she comes all over my cock. With one more deep thrust, my release feels endless, but it's been too long, too many days.

I curl around her, holding her from behind for several moments until I can straighten. When I withdraw, I look down to see her release and mine dripping out and down her thighs. The sight alone is enough to make me want her all over again.

My release was so powerful, I'm unsteady on my knees, and I have to grip the counter for a moment to gather myself. I press a trail of kisses down her spine and slowly ease back, straightening her dress and turning her to face me.

Her eyes are wide, her lips parted slightly. "I missed you," she says again.

Chapter Fourteen

MELODY

"Can you see?" the doctor asks.

I peer at the screen she's showing us. I know I'm pregnant because I can feel it. What started as almost a subtle hum inside has become a strong sense of presence.

Hunter stands next to where I'm seated on the exam table. "Wow," I breathe, looking at the shadowy shape in the image.

The doctor looks from me to Hunter. "There's your little baby," she says. "We can already see a little tail developing." She points at a blurry spot on the image.

When I look up at Hunter and see tears shining in his eyes, I feel like my heart might burst out of my chest. "I can't believe it!" I exclaim.

I look over at the doctor again while Hunter squeezes my hand. "I felt like I was pregnant, but I'm surprised that it happened so fast," I add.

The doctor taps through a few screens on her computer before facing me again. She grew up here and has a slender tail that flicks behind her as her intelligent gaze studies me. "Most women from Earth say that, but our research is clear. Human women become more fertile when they come to our planet.

Right now, our people need this," she says. "We're grateful you are willing to come here." The doctor shifts her focus to Hunter. "And how are you feeling, our father-to-be?"

"Very excited." He looks down at me. "But now I'm going to worry about Melody."

The doctor's chuckle is warm. "She'll be fine. She is very healthy, and the pregnancy is progressing as it should. All of her vital signs are strong. Do you have any questions for me before I go to my next patient?"

I shake my head. "I don't think so."

She dips her chin in acknowledgment. "Please schedule with the receptionist on the way out. We have a regular series of appointments for you. If anything comes up, all you have to do is page our office through your communicator. We have backup emergency services if needed. I don't anticipate you'll need that at any point, though."

With another smile, she slips out of the office. Hunter steps in front of me, letting his forehead fall to mine. "I love you." His voice is gruff.

"And I, you," I say.

He places a palm over my belly as he lifts his head. "I can already feel the curve. I've also noticed that your breasts are swelling."

His eyes drop to my breasts, and I giggle. He takes a quick breath. "I will try not to worry too much."

I place my palm over his where it rests on my belly. "You worry too much as it is. I'll be fine," I say.

That afternoon, Hunter has to go to work. In addition to monitoring the protesters, Earth has sent their first team of emissaries to our planet in decades. It's a big deal. Many have gathered at the governmental buildings to address this, and Jane is in meetings with them.

Nadine has told me she's having a support group this afternoon, so I decide to join her. I feel like I've adjusted to life here fairly well. I enjoy meeting with the women from Earth and feeling like I'm a part of something.

Nadine is already there with Romi, Risa, Hannah, Jenny, and Martha. When I sit down beside Romi, she smiles at me and waggles her brows. "Congratulations," she says in a sing-song voice.

"Is it official?" Nadine asks.

I nod. "Yes, I saw the doctor today with Hunter. I can't wait." I feel like I've been smiling for hours at this point.

"What's official?" Martha asks.

"I'm pregnant. I thought I was, but I wasn't ready to say anything about it until the doctor confirmed it. To be honest..." I pause, my gaze sobering. "When I lived on Earth, the last thing I wanted was to have a baby. I hoped to avoid men and family for the rest of my life. I can't believe how different I feel after just a few months here."

"Here, having a family is worth it," Nadine offers softly.

"It is," I agree.

Risa glances toward Romi. "And what about you? Have you met your mate yet?"

I expect Romi to shake her head and be dismissive, but when she hesitates and her cheeks turn pink, my mouth drops open. "Who?" I gasp.

"Tell us everything," Nadine teases. She gestures to the center of the table. "And, please, eat. I got the snacks from the coffee shop. Trudy made her special cookies, and the lemonade is, of course, from the lemon grove in town."

"Romi has been a little cynical about meeting anyone. We weren't sure she'd even want to find a mate," I explain to the newer women in our group as I take a cookie and a glass of lemonade.

Romi rolls her eyes. "I've been worried I wouldn't find a mate, but..." Pausing, she looks toward me. "When Hunter and his team returned to the stables, there was a man with them who

I hadn't seen yet." Her cheeks are bright red, and she pauses to take a swallow of lemonade.

"And?" Nadine circles her hand in the air impatiently.

Romi rolls her eyes again. "And, well, there was a vibe."

"A vibe or a pulse?" I prompt.

Romi sighs. "I don't know what the infinity pulse feels like, but I know this man wouldn't stop looking at me. He's the first alien I've met that I might want anything to do with. Well, not just alien man, but a man of any species—human, alien, or otherwise."

Nadine and I laugh together, along with the other women who join in.

Romi throws her hands up. "I can't help that I don't like men. I mean, Asher seems really nice, and Kayden worships the very ground you walk on, but still," she says dryly. Her eyes arc toward me. "Hunter worships you too, and it's strange to see." She looks toward the new women who've arrived from Earth. "The way the men here treat women is..." She sighs dramatically. "You'd think it was a joke. Even the couples who don't have the infinity pulse are good to each other. The men are respectful of women here. They're kind, and they protect them. The women are treated..."

When she pauses again, Nadine interjects, "Like equals."

"Yeah." Romi nods vigorously. "It's crazy."

"What's his name?" I ask, wondering if I've met the man Romi might like.

"Thorne. Hunter said that even though he's grumpy, he's a good man. It was kind of funny," Romi offers with a shrug. "Hunter saw us looking at each other."

"I've met Thorne," Nadine offers, her lips teasing with a smile. "He is on the broody side. I agree with Hunter that he can be a grump. I'll ask Kayden about him and get the whole scoop."

"Same," I offer. "If he was with Hunter, then he's on the team of spies. Hunter only works with those he trusts, so that's a good sign about Thorne."

"Can someone explain this whole spy thing to us?" Risa asks.

Nadine quickly summarizes the situation. "This planet is a democracy. They vote and everything, but they've always had a figurehead royal family. They keep it that way because it's a benevolent leadership, and the royal family protects the planet."

"It's one of the best planets in the galaxy," I add. "We have the best medical care here. We offer services all over the galaxy, even to Earth."

"Anyway, long story short, there's a small group in one town that has been protesting the line of succession in the royal family," Romi says.

I roll my eyes. "They say we shouldn't have a royal family, but they want to change the royal family succession so they can be part of it. Before Asher found Jane on Earth, he had to marry within a certain timeframe. He was running out of time. That's why they came to Earth. Although they've traveled to Earth for centuries. That's not anything new, but after so many women died in the big space storm during the festival to honor women, they came up with this plan to set up a matchmaking service with Earth. That's why we're all here."

Nadine picks up the thread. "Asher married in time, and Jane's already had a baby. The protesters kidnapped her, though, so now it's a big deal."

Jenny gasps.

"Women are much safer here than on Earth," I hurry to explain. "Jane wasn't harmed, but the spies that are part of the security for the royal family and the government are monitoring the situation in that town. There are new security protocols in place for all of us."

"The men who spy are some of the most trusted bodyguards in the royal security. Since Thorne is one of them, that's a good sign," Nadine adds. "We'll get the details on him. I know Melody will help me find out everything we need to know."

Romi looks between us, vulnerability and uncertainty flickering in her eyes. I smile over at her. "I want you to experience the infinity pulse, although I totally understand your perspective. I felt the same way. I thought if I could just get married and not have to worry about being beaten, that would be enough. I still believe that, but I hope for more for you too."

Romi startles me by leaning over and giving me a quick side hug. "Enough about me. Let's talk about something else," she announces a moment later.

Nadine is excited about her support group and launches into an introduction of why she wanted to start this. She even brings out a whiteboard, eliciting a chuckle from Romi.

Nadine grins over at her. "Hey, this will help us too. There's so much to learn." She glances among us. "So many different aliens travel to this planet because it's an intergalactic hub. This planet is respected by many others and provides support all over the galaxy. Until I arrived, I didn't know they'd provided food and other supplies to Earth for decades."

"I'm wondering about Earth finally traveling here," I chime in. "It's not like they don't travel at all, but they have shitty spaceships. Only the wealthiest of the wealthy can afford to travel. They certainly haven't sent a governmental emissary group anywhere recently."

"We don't freaking know how much people from Earth have traveled," Romi says bluntly. "I mean, sure, we know they haven't come here, but who would tell us back there? Here, there's news, and we have access to information. The only thing we had on Earth was GalaxyCosmo. I've learned more about Earth's history here than I did living on Earth. My mom was a teacher for a while, and my grandmother was too, so we had some old history books hidden, but there were missing pages." Romi shakes her head. She turns her focus to the new women in the group. "No matter what, life here will be better for you. Even though I worry, Jane promises us that you're safe here, even if you don't find a mate. I believe her."

"I do too. Also, if you decide you want to have kids but don't find a mate, they have a whole program for that. Trudy, an orc who lives here, and her wife plan to have a baby. Trudy is so excited," Nadine explains.

"What about jobs? We want to work," Risa says.

Nadine gets rolling with that question, happily using her whiteboard to list their options.

Chapter Fifteen

MELODY

When I return home that night, Hunter has prepared a feast for me. I've discovered he loves to cook. I look around at the amount of food on the table, and my heart feels like it will burst out of my chest with joy.

"This is a lot of food," I point out. "There's no way I can eat all this tonight."

"You're pregnant," he says, as if that explains everything.

"Um, yes, but only so much food will fit inside me."

Hunter's eyes dip from me down to the table and back again before a sheepish smile curls his lips.

I stop beside him and lean up to press a kiss on his cheek. "I love you for wanting to overfeed me," I tease.

I'm savoring this time with Hunter because he has to leave again. This time, he assures me it will only be a few days. Asher and Jane are traveling to another town on the planet, and the security detail is going with them. This is the town where the group of emissaries from Earth have traveled. I admit to being very curious about this group. I knew from growing up on Earth that even though it's been at least a century since Earth reigned supreme in the galaxy, there are still those there who believe Earth to be superior. Now that I'm here, I recognize how ridiculous that is. Of course, Earth did offer much to the galaxy once upon a time, but other planets also have many contributions.

Earth's history teaches the rest of the galaxy what it means to destroy your own environment. Jane has assured us she'll report back so we can hear all the gossip about the Earth group.

The morning before Hunter leaves, he studies me with worry flickering in his eyes. "Promise me you will contact the medical team if anything comes up," he says.

"Hunter, I've already promised you that. The doctor assures me I'm healthy and my pregnancy is going well." I lean up to give him a lingering kiss. "You need not worry."

I'm supposed to learn to ride the horses soon, but Hunter's asked me to wait until after I have the baby. I think that's a little ridiculous, but I'm willing to humor him. In the meantime, we have a chienne, this planet's version of a dog. She is sweet and loving with luxurious silver fur. Hunter wants me to have company when he's gone. I'm relieved she's here because the house feels so empty when he's not here. Back on Earth, all I wanted was to be alone.

"Promise me you'll be safe," I say as I hold his hands beside the mount he will ride to travel with the prince and others.

"Always," he says.

I watch as he mounts before taking to the air. When I'm home that night, I miss him.

Two days pass, and all is quiet. But that night, I feel the burning tug on what I think of as the cord that connects Hunter and me—our infinity pulse. I tell myself it just means they're traveling home because they're due home tomorrow.

Yet I feel a sense of uneasiness, and I'm grateful for our dog's comforting presence.

Chapter Sixteen

HUNTER

While the prince and princess meet with the emissary team from Earth, I know something is wrong. I catch Kayden's eyes, and he nods imperceptibly in return.

We activate the guard. It's a shield, invisible to anyone other than those on the security team and those we protect. Only moments later, our shared premonition proves true.

Thorne draws my attention, nudging his head to the side. I glance over to see a man we met during our information gathering in the town where the protesters are. Not for the first time, I'm relieved we made sure we went in disguise. Otherwise, our cover would be blown.

An emissary from Earth gestures toward the man. "He tells us you all are having undemocratic trials."

Asher's eyes narrow as he scoffs. "Absolutely not. However, we appreciate you revealing yet another man who's willing to threaten our planet's democracy. How dare you come here under false pretenses? Earth relies on our bounty and that of other planets to keep you and your people alive while you try to build that which you destroyed."

Thorne is standing at my side and speaks under his breath. "They have weapons."

In a flash, what is supposed to be a peaceful meeting turns into hand-to-hand fighting. Blessedly, we already have the shield up to prevent anyone else from trying to intervene, including what turned out to be three men from our planet.

The group from Earth appears shocked when our bodyguards surround them. Despite being able to quell this fight quickly, several of us have injuries, including me. I can feel the burning from the slice of a blade along my shoulder and arm. Thorne also sustained a wound. The prince is unscathed, but he is furious after we have subdued the men.

I ignore my injury, barking out orders along with Kayden. We are securing the spaceship that they traveled on to get here. The man who claims to be their leader is red-faced and furious, holding his chin up stubbornly. "You cannot just take our women," he says.

"Ah, so that's what this visit is about," I reply.

"We can. They are free to travel, and you know it. If you want the help from our planet and others in the galaxy, it will stay that way," Asher bites out.

Kayden, Thorne, and I leave Asher to talk and move our attention to deal with those from our planet. "We presume you've communicated with those from Earth," I say, my tone cold.

"What of it?" a man sneers. "We don't agree with mating with human women. It weakens us."

Kayden studies him. "I know who you are. Your own mother is human, and you have a sibling who is half orc. Do you hate yourself?"

The man sputters, his features twisting angrily. "None of that matters."

I catch Kayden's eye. "We will arrest them." I glance over toward Asher. "Meanwhile, we will have to reconsider any communication with Earth from now on. We know to be careful."

____

Despite my injury, I stay behind for several days to help. We have to handle the arrests and make plans to deal with the spaceship from Earth. I think I'm fine. My wound is just a nuisance that needs to heal. But by the evening before we are planning to leave, my arm is throbbing. I peel off my jacket to check and see the gash has become a deep shade of red.

Thorne sits beside me and glances over, his breath hissing through his teeth. "We need to get you home. Why didn't you say anything sooner?"

"Because it felt fine," I insist.

"Perhaps we should return tonight," he adds. "I can check. I'm sure we can rustle everyone up to leave sooner."

I examine the gash, which runs from my shoulder about halfway down my upper arm. "Where is our medic?" I ask.

Thorne taps his communicator faster than me and calls for our medic. We always travel with one. The medic eyes my wound. "Should've said something sooner," he mutters. "Now it's infected."

He douses it liberally with a burning disinfectant, and I ignore the stinging pain. "I'm going to stitch it up, but when we get back, you'll need a course of antibiotics. We don't know what bacteria might've been on their weapons."

Chapter Seventeen

MELODY

"Hunter's going to the medical center?" I yelp.

Helena nods. "He's one of several who sustained injuries. We think there might be a type of bacteria our people are not accustomed to."

"Can I see him?" I ask, trying to contain the fear and anxiety spinning wildly inside.

Helena presses her lips together, worry chasing in her gaze. "I understand you'd like to see him, but I recommend against it. You're about to give birth. We don't want you, or your baby, exposed to anything," she points out.

Alarm jolts through me. I press my palm to my chest as that anxiety and fear spin into a whirling storm inside. "How long do I have to wait?"

"The medical team is recommending a full week. He's not alone. All of those who sustained any injuries from the weapons from Earth are being quarantined together." Her tone is calm and matter-of-fact, a contrast to the way I feel inside.

"I'm due to give birth in a few days!" I exclaim.

Helena nods. "I'm aware. Princess Jane and Nadine can be with you for the birth. And Romi would like to come stay with you at your home if you're okay with that."

I blink back the tears welling in my eyes. "I would like that. Although I have my chienne, it's been lonely without Hunter."

"You can communicate with him," she assures me. "Now that he's close enough, your communicator will work."

I tap it immediately after Helena shows me how to select the hospital location on the small communicator. "Hunter!" I exclaim as soon as I hear his voice.

"Hi, sweetheart," he says, the low rumble of his voice making me feel warm inside.

Tears spring to my eyes again. "Are you okay? Helena told me you got injured."

"I'm fine," he says. "It's just a cut. The medical team thinks the infection is because of exposure to a type of earthly bacteria."

Relief rushes through me. "I miss you." I swallow through the thickness in my throat.

"As I miss you," he says.

Even though I want to see him right this very second, his calm tone soothes me. I feel the visceral tug between us even though we aren't in the same place.

"I love you, Melody, and I'll be waiting. The medical team says we'll be here for a week. They want to make sure we're all fully healed to prevent exposure to anyone else."

"Helena explained it to me. I understand, but I'm sad. I miss you, and I'm due to deliver our baby before the week is over."

"I know you are. I'm sorry this happened," he says.

I take a shaky breath. "It's your job."

"It is. Now we know we have to be more careful about any travelers from Earth. I'd like to talk every evening before you go to bed."

I take a slow breath. "I'd like that. We can text on our communicators too," I point out.

Texting isn't much of a habit here. It's kind of funny because they are so much more advanced than Earth, but they don't rely on that form of communication. Communication is more personal. I like that. I'd rather hear Hunter's voice.

"Please let me know when you go into labor, so the medical team here can keep me appraised. Maybe our baby will be late," he says hopefully.

I laugh softly. "I don't think so. She's kicking a lot. I feel like she's ready for the world," I say.

———

Romi comes to stay with me that evening, along with Risa. I've readied the extra bedroom we have for them to share. Romi plunks down on the couch, smiling over at me. "It's so funny to be here," she says.

"What's funny?" I ask.

"The whole time I lived on Earth, when I heard about how we used to have television and things, I was so envious of the past. That's all I wanted. Now, I know we can have it here." She gestures to the large screen mounted on the wall. "Yet I don't really think about it. I prefer spending time with people. It's nice."

"How are you feeling?" Risa asks.

I instinctively slide my hand over my belly, and our baby girl kicks in response. Emotion rises swiftly inside. "She has been busy these days," I say. "I feel like she's knocking on the door of my womb."

Risa laughs softly. "You are due soon, so that makes sense."

Romi takes a swallow of lemonade, tucking her feet under her knees as she looks over at me. "I know you're worried about Hunter, but he's going to be fine. They're all going to be fine. Leave it to the visitors from Earth to be assholes." She rolls her eyes.

I let out a sigh, nodding in agreement. "I know he's going to be fine. I've already talked to him twice, and we plan to talk every evening. I just can't believe the visitors from Earth would do that. They're risking their supplies and support from here."

Romi twists her mouth to the side. "I can believe it. They rely on the largesse of so many other planets, supplying food and more. They're upset over our people here coming up with a smart plan to recruit women to come here. They're just idiots, but we know that."

"I hope they will not try to take any of us back to Earth," Risa says, her eyes flickering with worry.

"I dare them to try," Romi says, lifting her chin, a dare flashing in her gaze. "I would have fun fighting them. As it is, they're going to pay a price for this. Any spaceships from Earth that try to visit here and other planets nearby will be subject to search and seizure. I heard they've also put a call out to the galaxy and any planets that support them."

"It's amazing how much we didn't know on Earth," I muse.

"Yeah, we thought the green zone existed because of Earth's government trying to rebuild. Come to find out, they just hoard the help they get," Risa says, her tone laced with a hint of bitterness.

We continue talking for a little while until I feel an abrupt pain. It's intense enough that Romi and Risa notice my wince.

"Oh, is that a contraction?" Romi suddenly looks panicked.

"Maybe?" I shrug, trying to play it cool. "My doctor told me I might feel some contractions days before I go into actual labor," I explain.

Romi and Risa keep me occupied over the next few hours. I'm so grateful they're there.

The contractions increase in intensity later that evening. Despite my assurances that this is just a false alarm, I eventually admit I must be in labor. Our daughter is in a rush to enter this world.

I want to contact Hunter first, but Romi looks at me like I'm crazy and calls the medical team. The next few hours pass in a blur.

Although I want to talk with Hunter through the entirety of giving birth, the nurse points out I can't talk easily, and I should focus on the baby. Romi stays with me through my labor, giving me support and encouragement. Nadine and Jane are also there to help. After the birth is over and our little girl is curled up safe and swaddled in a soft blanket, the medical team sets up a call for me on a screen in the hospital room.

It's the first time I've seen Hunter since he left to travel with the royal team. He looks a little rough around the edges. His hair is rumpled, his bronzed skin looks pale, and his brow is creased with worry.

"Hunter! She's healthy." I gesture to our baby girl.

We've already selected a name. We're naming her Emily, after my mother.

His lips curl in a slow smile as his eyes coast over my face. "How are you feeling?" he asks.

"I'm tired, but I'm fine," I say.

"Your little girl came early," Romi calls out from the corner of the room where she's sitting in a chair. "Melody was amazing, and the birth went great."

Hunter chuckles. "I'm glad to hear it." He holds my gaze. "I love you."

"I love you too. I know you'll be out of the hospital soon. Even though I miss you and I'm sad you're not right here with us, I want you to be safe and completely healthy."

His eyes hold mine, and I feel the tug of our connection. "Soon," he promises me.

Chapter Eighteen

HUNTER

Two months later

I find myself frequently checking on Melody and our baby girl. They are safe, and we are all healthy. Those of us who sustained superficial injuries from the fighting with the visitors from Earth are all healthy. Our medical scientists are studying the bacteria that caused the infections, but thus far, it has caused no further issues.

I've been out of the hospital for over two months now and savor every moment with Melody and our baby girl. She is healthy and strong, just like her mother.

We are home one afternoon, and Melody finishes nursing. I can't help the surge of desire when I look over her. Her breasts are plump and full. She glances my way as she stands, pulling her dress back up over her breasts. Her cheeks turn pink when she sees me watching.

"I'll be right back," she says. "I'm going to put Emily down for her nap."

As she walks down the hallway, I watch the swing of her hips. A few minutes later, she returns to the living room, and I beckon her over to me. She crosses the room to stand in front of me where I'm seated on the couch. I ache for her.

Her eyes lock with mine, and our connection pulses between

us, sizzling with the power of our desire. She steps between my knees, and I curl my fingers on the soft, stretchy collar of her dress and tug it down. Her breasts spill out. I lean forward to suck on one nipple, then the other. Her skin flushes pink with passion, and she lets out a little whimper when I lean back.

I cup both breasts and tease my thumbs over her now damp nipples. "Are you wet for me, sweetheart?" I murmur.

She shifts restlessly on her feet, and I know the answer. I release her breasts, leaning back to swiftly free my length. Cum is already rolling out and down my swollen shaft. Melody's lips are parted. Her tongue darts out, and she licks her lips.

"Take your dress off," I say.

She steps back and lifts it over her head, where it falls in a rumple on the floor behind her. I love the sweet curves of her body. I savor the little stretch marks along her belly and hips, reminding me of how she carried our baby. She straddles my knees, and I look down. She's wet for me. I tease my fingers through her folds, gratified as she lets out a little moan when I circle my fingertip around her swollen nub that's poking out.

"Ride me," I say.

She does as I ask, rising a little. I feel the slick kiss of her entrance on my thick crown. We watch together when she slowly rolls her hips down, sheathing me in her clenching core. I hold her close, fucking her slowly. I know her body now. I know when she's beginning to find her release as she trembles and shudders around me.

I fill her with my own release when she collapses against me. She leans back a few moments later. I kiss her. "I love you, and I always will," I tell her, just like I do every day.

Fury, my favorite horse, snorts before lowering his head. He's stunning with his shimmery golden coat.

I look up at him. "You are proud, aren't you?" I tease. He snorts again, and I stroke my hand along the side of his neck.

The horses here are like Earth horses, but they can fly. Like the aliens here, they have descended from a combination of species. The people here are descendants of cowboys from Earth who traveled through the galaxy centuries ago. The offspring they created is stronger and healthier than humans and the original aliens.

The horses the cowboys brought with them mated with horses native to this planet that were dying out at the time. Now, these beautiful creatures are here. I feel lucky to have a job where I help care for them and train them. On Earth, I was basically a slave. I worked in the stables there as well. Even though I was tired all the time, I loved my job.

On this new planet, I have much more freedom with my job and am treated with respect. I feel goose bumps rise on my skin and a little tug in my chest. I think I know who's close by, but I'm not sure, and I'm almost afraid to turn around. Not out of genuine fear but because this feeling is so unsettling. My skin starts to feel hot.

"Romi," a male voice says, the sound sizzling through my body and making my belly feel funny and liquid inside.

I turn, lifting my chin. I've seen this man before. I know his name is Thorne, and he is part of the royal security team and an elite spy. I've gathered that information from my friends. He has the golden eyes all the alien cowboys have here and gorgeous bronze skin that shimmers under this planet's sun.

My heart beats faster like hooves pounding on the ground inside my body. My breath is shallow, and my knees feel wobbly.

"Hi," I say, my voice breathless.

He takes a step closer, and I see his tail twitch behind him. I feel an unfamiliar liquid sensation between my thighs. Thorne's eyes narrow as he takes another step closer, and I can hardly breathe as I stare up at him. For a human woman, I am tall. But these alien cowboys tower over me, and it makes me feel vulnerable in a way I don't like.

I have fought for all of my life to simply stay alive on Earth. That familiar survival instinct is still there, rearing its presence. "I'm Thorne," he says. "You are Romi." He pauses, his intent golden gaze sweeping over me. "And you are mine."

The finality in his tone is startling. I stare at him, feeling my lips part as those pounding hooves gather force inside my chest.

"I am?" My voice sounds distant and unfamiliar to me, breathy and uncertain.

Thorne nods as he takes yet another step closer. I fear I might legit swoon. Swooning is not a thing I do. I grew up hating men. Men on Earth are cruel. It's a little strange and unsettling to watch how women are worshipped here, to watch friends of mine fall deeply in love.

Thorne lifts his hand, palming my cheek. His thumb traces along my jaw, the calloused surface of it sending sparks over my skin. He drags it across my lip. I can feel a visceral pull to step closer. I have never wanted someone's touch. Ever. Much less a man's.

Right now, this very second, I want his mouth on mine. I want him to mark me.

Just then, I hear another voice. Startled, I jump back. When I look over my shoulder, I see the prince and princess, Asher and Jane, approaching. Thorne appears entirely unaffected by their presence. He steps back. "Can I have a moment alone with Romi?" he asks the prince.

Asher looks toward Jane, and I see the questions swirling in his gaze. I still find it so strange that he defers to her. Jane, who is also my friend and who I care for deeply, narrows her eyes at Thorne before looking toward me.

"Would you like a moment with Thorne?" she asks. "He has told the prince he would like you as a mate."

My heart is still pounding at a frenetic gallop in my chest. When I look up at Thorne, I know that this man is meant to be my mate. I look back at Jane and swallow through my nervousness. "Okay," I say.

Thorne reaches for my hand, his big palm engulfing mine. He leads me down the breezeway in the barn and into a small room where we keep equipment and supplies. I walk on wobbly knees as the door clicks shut behind us.

Thorne has not released my hand, and he turns to face me. I bump into him. His arm slides around my waist to steady me. His body is hard and strong, and I feel so small beside him. His eyes bore into mine as he moves, nudging me backward until my hips bump a table.

Without even asking, he lifts me and slides my hips on it. "I'm going to kiss you now," he states. "Is that okay?"

I want it more than anything, but I can't speak, so I nod. Following an unsteady breath, his mouth is on mine. His kisses are slow and sensual, and I feel like I'm melting inside. I'm relieved that I'm sitting on this table. Otherwise, I know I'd collapse.

I feel him dragging my dress up around my hips. He steps back, and all I can do is look up at him. He reaches for my hand and places it over the front of his breeches. I feel the heat of his hard shaft pulsing underneath my touch.

"I want you. We will have to wait, but first, I will give you a taste," he says.

I don't even know what he means just now, but I want it. He reaches around my waist, his palm splaying at the base of my spine. He nudges my hips forward until my legs dangle. He cups his palm between my thighs, right where I feel an unfamiliar ache and a heaviness that I've never experienced.

He teases his fingers over the fabric there as he asks, "Have you had a man before?"

I shake my head. In a blink, he has pushed my panties out of the way and is teasing his fingers between my thighs where I'm dripping wet. All I know is that this feels so good. So, so good.

I want something to fill me, but he doesn't give me that except for once when he presses two fingers inside just as he teases his thumb over a swollen place. A sense of pleasure explodes through me, and I hear myself calling his name.

He shocks me even further as he withdraws his fingers and swiftly unbuttons his breeches. "Watch," he tells me.

I look down to see white liquid rolling out at the tip of his length. He smears his fingers over the top of it before lifting them to my mouth. I suck my arousal and his off his fingers, hearing myself moan at the tangy, salty flavor.

His eyes are dark. "We will mate in a week," he declares.

I stare up at him as his lips descend to mine again. I hear myself letting out a little sigh into our kiss. All I know is I need more, and waiting for it feels like forever.

When he lifts his head, he asks, "Will you be mine?"

Thank you for reading Hunter & Melody's story - I hope you loved it!

If you'd like a glimpse from their future, you can join my newsletter to receive an exclusive scene.

Sign up here: https://BookHip.com/XGMNCSX

Up next in the Match Made in Space Series is Fate for the Space Cowboy. When Romi takes off for a new planet, she's planning on not being anyone's mate. You know what they say about the best laid plans though. When she locks eyes with Thorne, a tall, enigmatic alien cowboy bodyguard, all bets are off. Buckle up for more space cowboy spice!

One-click to pre-order: Fate for the Space Cowboy - due out June 2025!

Sign up for my newsletter, so you can receive information about upcoming new releases & deals: https://phoebebelle.com/

ABOUT THE AUTHOR

Phoebe Belle lives on Earth. She loves escaping into happily-ever-afters, her family - human, canine and maybe even alien (not willing to rule that out because you never know!) - coffee and cooking.

https://phoebebelle.com/

facebook.com/phoebebellegalaxyromance
instagram.com/phoebebellegalaxyromance